# TED AND HIS TIME-TRAVELLING TOILET

# ROMAN REWIND

## BY
## STEVEN VINACOUR

AWARD PUBLICATIONS LIMITED

ISBN 978-1-78270-384-6

Text copyright © 2019 Steven Vinacour
Illustrations by James Cottell
This edition copyright © Award Publications Limited

First published by Award Publications Limited 2020

Published by Award Publications Limited,
The Old Riding School, Welbeck,
Worksop, S80 3LR

www.awardpublications.co.uk

201

Printed in the United Kingdom

MIX
Paper from
responsible sources
FSC® C020471

# WARNING:
## CONTAINS TOILET HUMOUR!

YOU →

# CHAPTER 1

I'm Ted and I have a secret. Actually, I have two secrets. The first one is just a normal, ordinary secretive kind of secret. The other, on the scale of secrets, with one being a teeny, tiny little secret and ten being the most humungous, jaw-dropping, pant-wettingly enormous secret – this is definitely a ten... and a bit.

If I were to come straight out and just tell you the secret then it's possible that the shock of hearing it could cause your

5

head to pop off your shoulders like a cork from a bottle. I would feel very guilty if that happened to you and I'd have to answer very ANGRY emails from your parents telling me that I caused your head to pop off, fly out the window, land on a passing lorry and be carried off never to be seen again. No one wants that.

So, I'll start by telling you the little secret first and we will just have to see how well you cope. First you have to promise never to tell anyone...

... promise?

... really promise?

... really, really, really promise?

OK, I'll tell you. Come a bit closer ...

... closer ...

... even closer ...

THAT'S TOO CLOSE!

Back up a bit.

Too far ...

Take half a step forward ...

Hmmm... take a quarter of a step backwards.

There... stop... OK. Now, before I tell you, you also have to promise that you won't laugh. You won't, will you? And when I say laugh I also mean giggle, chuckle, chortle, cackle, snigger, smile, guffaw and titter.

All right then. Ready?

Shhhhh...

Here goes...

My name isn't really Ted!

I know, right? Mind blowing!

Let me explain.

I re-named myself Ted as soon as I turned ten. I decided on Ted because it was the shortest name I could possibly think of which was the exact opposite of my real name which, thanks to my parents, is the stupidest, most ridiculously long name in the whole entire world. They decided to name me the most stupidest, longest, most ridiculously long name in the whole entire world because they thought it would give me character. In fact, all it gave me was a sore hand whenever I wrote my name on my homework! So, if you promise not to laugh I will tell you my full name …

… promise?

Really, really, truly, hand-on-heart promise?

OK, here goes…

My full name is Terry Barry Larry Gary Harry Jerry Perry Lenny Benny Johnny Tommy Julie Jones.

Are you laughing? Because you promised not to.

The problem is that my parents are hopeless at making decisions. Some nights they spend so long making up their minds what they want for supper that it's time for breakfast. So, when my mum was pregnant with me, they made a list of all the names they liked and then couldn't decide which one to give me, so they gave them all to me. At that time, they also didn't know if I was going to be a girl or a boy. If I turned out to be a girl, I would've just been named Julie as that is the only girl's name they liked. When I turned out to be a boy they felt it was a shame to waste such a lovely name (bleugh) and so they put it on the end. Typical isn't it? The only quick decision they ever made and it was the wrong one!

9

The last time I heard my full name was when I got myself into trouble for 'accidently' repainting my school trousers. Grey is such a **boring** colour and I thought green stripes would work this season. When I noticed that I'd also managed to get green paint all over my bed sheets, I knew I'd be in double trouble. So, when my mum stood at the bottom of the stairs with her hands on her hips and shouted, 'Terry Barry Larry Gary Harry Jerry Perry Benny Johnny Tommy Julie Jones, come down here at once!' I knew what was coming.

I didn't move. She called again and again. Finally, she marched up the stairs and burst in through my door knocking over a pile of comics I'd just sorted out.

'Why didn't you answer me when I called?'

she shouted.

I pointed out her mistake at once.

'You missed out Lenny.'

'What?' she replied.

'You missed out Lenny. My name is Terry Barry Larry Gary Harry Jerry Perry Lenny Benny Johnny Tommy Julie Jones, and <u>you</u> said Terry Barry Larry Gary Harry Jerry Perry Benny Johnny Tommy Julie Jones, which technically isn't my name so I couldn't be sure that it was me you were calling.'

Mum stood in the doorway counting out my names on her fingers. I waited for her to realise that she had made the mistake. I went back to reading my comic until she had figured it out.

'Right, well anyway... <u>You</u> are in big trouble, young man. What on earth were you thinking? Painting your school trousers with green stripes? And you've ruined your bed sheets!'

'I was being creative, Mum. I was thinking outside the box.'

'What box?' asked Mum.

'The box, not a box,' I explained. Mum scratched her head and looked confused.

'You don't have a box.'

'I know, but if I did...' I replied.

'But you don't!' she argued.

'BUT IF I DID!'

'How big is it? Where would you keep it? Your room is full of junk. Put the junk in the box.'

'What box?' I asked.

'The box?' she said.

'What box?'

Now we were both confused about the

box that we don't have, and Mum had **completely** forgotten why she came upstairs in the first place so I avoided getting told off about the green striped school trousers.

Now, let's move on to the second secret. This is the big one. And when I say big, I mean

# BIG!

In order for me to tell you, we are going to have to go somewhere completely safe where no one could possibly hear what I say. I was thinking under my bed or in my wardrobe, but if Mum comes in again and finds me hiding in my wardrobe or under my bed with a complete stranger, then **questions** are going to be asked. So, there is only one option left. You take this book somewhere quiet and double check that no one is listening then I'll tell you.

It's OK, I'll wait...

Ready?

Double check again that no one is listening. Just in case. OK, here goes... I have a **TIME-TRAVELLING** toilet!

Shhhh!

Don't say anything. Just let the pant-dropping awesomeness of what I just told you sink in slowly and then I'll tell you all about it in a little while.

Sit down, calm down, maybe even go to the toilet. You know, your normal, ordinary non-time-travelling toilet. Unlike mine which is time-travelling.

Did I mention that?

Oh no, you've become all excited again.

Sit down (again). Calm down (again).

I'll be back in a minute.

# CHAPTER 2

Right then, I'm just going to come out with it.
I'll then give you a few moments to think
about what I've told you and then I'll try to
explain it all to you.

(Ahem.)

My **toilet** allows me to travel back in
time.

You're right.

I do now need to explain a little bit more.

A little while ago, I discovered that if I
stand in the toilet, think about a period in

history and then flush it, I **whizz** round and round at super high speed, disappear down the bowl, round the U-bend and then appear during the exact time I was thinking about. Now, as I let the awesomeness of my incredible news sink in, I should answer the obvious question that I know you've been thinking.

How did I first discover my terrific toilet's TIME-TRAVELLING abilities?

Well, funny story. You may wonder what I was hoping to achieve the first time I climbed into the toilet and flushed it. Let's just say that I won the game of Hide-and-Go-Seek that day. Please also bear in mind that if you like a game of Hide-and-Go-Seek and decide to also stand in the toilet bowl and press the flush button the only thing you will get is wet feet!

Time-travelling is not a standard function of your average toilet. My toilet is special, one-of-a-kind and until today no one in the world knew about its **amazing** abilities. It's now a secret between you, me and the toilet and I'd really like it if you kept it that way.

So, there you go, now you know. Is your mind blown? Did your head pop off? Did your pants **EXPLODE?**

The best thing about being able to travel through time is that I am really good at History in school. Which is a relief because I am not very good at any other subject. My school report reads like this:

**STAGE MOUNT SCHOOL REPORT**

| PUPIL | Ted Jones |
|---|---|
| **SUBJECT** | **COMMENTS** |
| **MATHEMATICS** | Not very good |

| | |
|---|---|
| **ENGLISH** | Not very good |
| **P.E.** | Not very good |
| **GEOGRAPHY** | Not very good |
| **SCIENCE** | Not very good |
| **HISTORY** | Really good |

Perhaps I would be better at lessons if other things in my bathroom had abilities. Maybe I could be **Ted and His Times Tables Tub.** I could disappear down the plughole of my bath and become a mathematics genius. Or I could be **Ted and His Clever Chemistry Cabinet** (this would work better if my name was Clive, which it isn't. So it doesn't. Anyway, stay with me.) I'd climb into the bathroom cabinet and be magically transported into a science lab where I'd create really important experiments. Or maybe I'd sit in a bidet and... work out what a bidet is actually used for. Unfortunately, I haven't tested these ideas out because I can't fit in the bathroom cabinet.

I've tried. I can't.

Even though I've waited until the very last drop of water has been sucked down the plughole I haven't even managed to follow it down past my little toe, which got stuck and Mum had to call the fire brigade who fell about laughing at me and after freeing me, told me not to stick my toe in anything like that again. So far I have listened to their advice.

I haven't ever sat in a bidet because I don't know what a bidet is. Hang on, I'll look it up...

# OH MY GOODNESS!

It's a mini bath for washing your **bottom!** Why would anyone need a bath that specifically washes their **bottom?** I don't have one that specifically washes my ears or my knees. **EWWWWWWWW!** That would be one tap I would not drink from. **YUCK.**

So now you know how I discovered that my toilet is special, I will now try to answer some of the other questions that I imagine you have.

**Your question:** Is <u>my</u> toilet suitable for time travel?

**My answer:** Probably not. Standing in a toilet and flushing it will do nothing but ruin your socks. Your

toilet is for toilet-y business and
nothing else. Sorry about that.

**Your question:** What happens when
someone uses <u>your</u> toilet for just doing
toilet-y business?

**My answer:** Well that is a good
question and one that I have often
wondered. To be honest, there is no
way of knowing unless you happen
to be reading a history book and
look really closely at a photograph
and notice a little puddle of pee or
a stray poo. I have studied all the
books in my library and so far, I've
seen nothing, although it did lead
to me being banned from my local
library. This is what happened:
(I'll write it like a play for added

drama and excitement!)

## Scene 1: INSIDE A LIBRARY

**Librarian** (<u>cheerfully</u>): Hello, can I help you?

**Ted:** Hello, I'd like a book please.

**Librarian:** Of course, young man. What sort of book would you like?

**Ted:** (<u>politely</u>) A history book please.

**Librarian:** Are you looking for anything in particular?

**Ted:** Yes. A poo. Specifically, one of mine. <u>(Librarian looks shocked, stands very still, mouth open.)</u>

Let's just say when she got over the shock the only thing she showed me was the door. Next question please.

**Your question:** Can anyone else travel back in time using your toilet?

**My answer:** Possibly, although I have yet to ask anyone as I don't trust anyone enough. There's a girl called *Chloe* in my class at school that I have a crush on. I trust her, but I don't think she will respond well to the chat-up line 'Do you want to come to my house and stand in the toilet with me? I'll even let you flush it.'

**Your question:** How do you get back from your time-travelling adventures?

**My answer:** There is only one way to get back. I have to close my eyes, hold my breath for three seconds, raise my right arm in the air and

pump it up and down like I'm flushing
a chain. Then, I open my eyes
and I'm back in my bathroom. Plus,
here's the best bit, no matter how
long I spend in the past, time seems
to stand still in the present, which
means no one in my house even
knows I'm gone.

**Your question:** When you flush the toilet and
whizz round and round do you ever shout
'WEEEEEEEEE'?

**My answer:** I'm not sure you are
taking the idea of magical toilets
seriously enough.

   Next question.

**Your question:** Can your toilet take you into
the future?

**My answer:** What? Don't be so daft; toilets can't take you into the future! Who's ever heard of such a crazy idea?

**Your question:** Well what if your toilet was in Australia where the water flushes down in the opposite direction? That could make you go into the future.

**My answer:** But my toilet isn't in Australia. And there is no way that I could take it to Australia! Imagine!

**Nice lady at the airport check-in desk:** Did you pack your suitcase yourself?

**Me:** Yes I did.

**Nice lady at the airport check-in desk:** It seems very heavy. Does it contain

anything dangerous or prohibited
items?

**Me:** Not unless you consider a toilet a
prohibited item.

**Nice lady at the airport check-in desk:**
A toilet? Why would you be carrying a
toilet in your suitcase?

**Me:** I got a plumber to disconnect my
toilet, then I packed it in my suitcase
and once I get to Australia I will find an
Australian plumber to connect it back
up again. Then, due to the fact that I am
now the other side of the world – in the
Southern Hemisphere where the water
swirls in the opposite direction to the
Northern Hemisphere, I can then stand
in the bowl, pull the chain and see if it
takes me off into the future.

**Was a nice lady at the airport check-**

**in desk but not a nice lady anymore (although she is still at the check-in desk):** HELP! I NEED SECURITY! AND POSSIBLY A NURSE!

So, as you can see, it's a silly question, I don't ask you if you've ever taken your bath on holiday, do I? Or have you ever taken your sink to school? No, of course not. I can't take my toilet to another country so we will never know.

I'll allow one more question. Please make it a sensible one. Thank you.

**Your question:** When you return from the past, do you ever look flushed?

**My answer:** RIGHT, THAT'S IT! NO MORE QUESTIONS!

Hopefully now I have answered all your

**27**

*sensible* questions and you are totally comfortable with the idea of time-travelling toilets. Some people read books or play computer games on the toilet. I travel back in time. No big deal. Get over it.

I'll tell you more later on, but for now I have to get ready for school. I'm hoping that today is a good day and I get to sit next to Chloe.

Actually, thinking about your question earlier. If I did have a toilet that let me travel into the future, I would definitely **whizz** forward in time and see if we get married – which I am pretty sure we will. I'm guessing we will start making wedding plans straight after I pluck up the courage to actually speak to her. I'm not usually shy but Chloe is the most beautiful girl in the school so whenever I see her I forget what it is I'm meant to say and just stare at her. As and when I do pluck up the courage to have a conversation with her, I know it will go well because the best thing is that we have something in common – we share the problem of having an embarrassing name. I would never actually tell her that she has an embarrassing name. That would be rude, and, let's be honest, she'd hardly fall in love with me if the first thing I said to her was:

'Oi, your name is a bit embarrassing, isn't it?'

Her full name is Chloe Louise Onions. ONIONS! As in... onions. If I had that surname, I would cry (that's the only onion-related joke I could think of – it's a good one

29

though, right? No? Oh well.) My one concern
is that when we do finally get to the wedding
day, this will happen:

'*Do you, Terry Barry Larry Gary
Harry Jerry Perry Lenny Benny
Johnny Tommy...*
(laughter from the congregation)
*...Julie...*
(more laughter from the congregation)
*...Jones take Chloe Louise Onions*
(everyone rolling around on the floor
laughing, including the vicar who can't
continue because he is laughing so hard)
*...to be your wife?*'

So, back to the conversation that we
haven't had but definitely will have
one day, I realise that I'd have to be subtle

and clever about bringing up the subject of having an embarrassing name, like...

> **Me**: Oh, Chloe, Onions is such an interesting surname. Where's it from?
> **Chloe**: The vegetable aisle in the supermarket.

Perhaps not.

Anyway, I'll worry about that nearer the time. Right now, I need to get to school.

LOOK AT ME!

# CHAPTER 3

Dad drops me off outside the school just as the head teacher, Mr Munford, starts to close the gates.

'Hurry up, young man! You're late!' he bellowed.

I was about to explain that the only reason we were running late was because my dad (who, you may remember I told you, can't make a quick decision... ever) was trying to decide what colour tie to wear. He ended up choosing a really **disgusting** multi-coloured mess of a tie that looked like a rainbow had been sick all down his shirt. On the journey to school he kept admiring himself in the car mirror. I just slunk down in my seat and hoped no one would see him and connect him to me.

I decided not to say anything and when Dad pulled up outside the school gates I stepped out of the car in silence.

Suddenly, my thoughts were interrupted by the school bully, Martin Harris, barging into me as he walked past. He was nearly twice as big as me and he very nearly knocked me over. Mr Munford called his name but he wasn't listening or chose not to answer.

Martin was *always* looking for trouble and was best avoided at all costs. I walked really slowly until he had gone far enough ahead of me. On the plus side it meant I was bruise free. On the down side I was now late for class.

I **RAN** through the corridor and skidded to a halt as I got to my classroom door. I had just enough time to throw my schoolbag, which landed in a perfect heap right by my chair, and join the back of the line as we were marched towards the school hall for (yawn) morning assembly.

Guess who was standing in front of me? Go on, guess...

Father Christmas? NO! Why would Father Christmas be standing in front of me waiting to go into my school assembly? Come on, be serious. Look, don't worry, I'll tell you... *Chloe!* What do you mean Chloe who? You know! Chloe – Chloe Onions! Oh, I get it – you just wanted me to say her surname so that you could laugh. Well, I'm not impressed, that's not funny. That's my future wife you are laughing at and I'd appreciate it if you could act much more maturely and when I say her name you say something like...

**'Oh yes, Ted, what a delightful and completely unfunny name. Please carry on with your completely fascinating and interesting story.'**

So, with that in mind, I'll just pretend that you said that to me and I'll carry on with my interesting story.

Where was I? Oh yes, standing in front of me was Chloe, which was the good news. But, here's the bad news: standing in front of her was her best friend Sandra Wum, who everyone calls **Sandy Bum** which is really funny – even funnier than Chloe Onions (which isn't funny). Actually, when I say everyone calls her that, I mean me and my best friend Ollie. Sandy Bum is *NOT* someone I get on with because she acts like the class police and always tells on anyone who is doing anything that they shouldn't be doing. She also says 'like' a lot. Which is ironic because I don't 'like' her.

So, ignoring Sandra, I put on my best smile ever and said, 'Hi Chloe.' But, she didn't hear me because Sandy and Chloe were talking... and talking... and talking... and talking. All they ever do is talk! I have no idea what they find to talk about. I don't think I know enough words to be able to talk as much as they talk. When I see my best friend Ollie I say, 'All right, Ollie,' and he

36

says, 'All right, Ted,' and then, that's about it.
Conversation over. Enough has been said.
Neither of us have anything else that <u>NEEDS</u>
to be added. It's a perfect conversation.

So anyway, I tried a couple of times to get
Chloe's attention but it was impossible.
I don't even think I would've got her to notice
me if I had taken my school shirt off and
waved it around my head whilst standing on
a box and shouting into a megaphone, 'Look
at me! Look at me! Over here! I'm
Ted your future husband, look at
me!'

So, instead, I stood quietly in line and
followed, feeling invisible to my one true
love.

That morning there was a guest speaker
in our assembly but I couldn't tell you what
he (or she) was talking about because I

wasn't concentrating as my mind was on other things. I'd decided that when I got home from school I was going to go on my next **TIME-TRAVELLING** adventure and I was too excited thinking about where I should go.

I could go millions and millions of years back in time to see the dinosaurs or I could go ten minutes back in time and stand in line for assembly, <u>actually</u> take my shirt off, wave it around my head and shout, 'Look at me, look at me!' into a megaphone at Chloe.

However, I think, given the choice, and fearing that it wouldn't be Chloe that notices me, but it would be Sandy Bum who turns around, falls in love with me and then decides to talk at me non-stop until we are both really, really old, I think my

chances of survival may be better with the
dinosaurs.

I finish my daydream just in time to hear
Mr Munford say, '... and that's why this half-
term holiday the whole school will be doing
a project on **THE ROMANS** for their
homework. I, along with your teachers, will
expect to see some impressive fact-filled
projects when we return. This time we are
going to offer a **prize** for the best project
but, to encourage you to hand it in on time,
I will expect them all to be handed in by 9:30
on the first Monday that we are back. Any
student that hands their project in late will
not be eligible for the prize. So, work hard,
don't forget to bring it in on time and good
luck to you all.'

I happen to look over at Chloe and see her
turn to Sandy Bum and whisper, 'Yes! I love

learning about the Romans.'

So I quickly say, 'I love learning about **THE ROMANS** too.' Except I forget that I'm in assembly and said it much too loudly and now, everyone has heard me and the whole hall has gone really quiet and everyone has turned to look at me.'

Mr Munford is glaring at me. 'Did you say something, young man?'

'Ummm... I said... I love learning about the Romans... umm... too.' I stutter as everyone in the hall starts to giggle.

'Good,' booms Mr Munford. 'I look forward to seeing your project. I expect it to be on time, unlike <u>you</u> most mornings, Mr Jones.'

'Yes, sir.' I sigh and my cheeks turn bright red as the whole school starts to giggle at my expense. This morning is a disaster.

I wanted to be noticed by Chloe and instead I've been noticed by the entire school (except Chloe who is still talking to Sandy). Today can only get better and it will, trust me, because I am going to produce the best project ever in the whole history of the school and I'm going to hand it in on time and win the prize because as soon as I get home, I've decided that I'm going back in time, to meet THE ROMANS.

# CHAPTER 4

As soon as the bell rings, I am out the door and **RUNNING** across the playground towards the school gates. Nothing will stop me getting home as quickly as possible.

Not even Chloe getting down on one knee and asking me to marry her.

Not even Mr Munford making me head boy and ruler of the school.

Not even if aliens flew down and kidnapped Sandy Bum and took her off to a distant planet never to be seen again.

(Well, OK, I **might** stop for a second, give them a round of applause and then carry on running, but that's all.)

**Wait,** back up. I just had a thought. Chloe might actually read this one day and now I've said that if she got down on one knee and asked me to marry her I'd say **no**. Just in case this happens I need to put a special note to Chloe. If you are not Chloe, or if you are *a* Chloe but not *the* Chloe then there is no need to read (ooh that rhymes) the following letter.

Dear Chloe,

How are you? Earlier on, you may have noticed that I wrote that if you were to go down on one knee and ask me to marry you, I would say no due to the fact that I was keen to get home as quickly as possible.

If you are considering asking me to marry you, then even if I was in a big hurry to get home, like, if something really important and amazing was happening at my house (it never does but just imagine that it was), then I would still stop and <u>definitely</u>, 100%, without a doubt say <u>yes</u> to marrying you because you are the best-looking girl in the school and you are AWESOME.

Please don't get embarrassed because everyone else reading this book has promised not to read this letter and I completely and utterly trust them.

Lots of Love,

Ted

XOXO

I burst through our front door and **CHARGED** up the stairs dropping my coat, bag, shoes, jumper, tie and lunchbox all the way to my room.

'Is that you, Ted?' called my mum from the kitchen.

'No!' I shouted back.

'Oh, OK,' she yelled back. 'Well whoever you are, do you want a snack?'

Excellent!

Taking tasty provisions on a trip back in time was always a good idea.

I grabbed as many snacks as I could hold without Mum getting *suspicious* and ran back to my room. I picked up my tablet and turned it on. Before I head down the loo on any trip (I know, even saying it sounds weird but it's true) I like to look up some information about where I'm going. Here's what I found out:

45

Romans came to Britain from Rome in Italy over 2,000 years ago.

They called London, Londinium.

They created lots of things like the design of our coins, central heating and even flushing toilets. So, if it wasn't for the Romans I'd never have discovered time travel. It seems that I have a lot to thank them for.

Well, they sound like an interesting bunch. Time to do some **toilet**-related travelling I think. I turned off my computer and crept into the bathroom remembering to lock the door. The last thing I want is for someone to walk in and see me climbing into the toilet!

Can you imagine?

'Ted, what on earth are you doing?'

'I'm... ummm... rehearsing for a school play.'

'You are standing in the toilet! What play could you possibly be rehearsing for?'

'Ummm... It's a Shakespeare play.'

'Which Shakespeare play requires you to stand barefoot in a toilet bowl?'

'Umm... Romeo and Poo-liet?'


That's a conversation I *don't* want to have, so I double-checked the lock again. I carefully removed my socks, lifted the lid and stepped into the cold water. I said the magic words – **I'M KIDDING!** Who do you think I am, Harry Potter? I closed my eyes (I don't actually *need* to do this and

**47**

don't do it every time I just sometimes get nervous about what I might see when being flushed down the **toilet** – if you know what I mean... ).

I reached out, pressed the flush and held my breath whilst saying, 'London, Roman times, London, Roman times, London, Roman times', over and over in my head.

# CHAPTER 5

Whenever I travel back in time, the experience is always similar – and trust me, it is always really cool. In fact, it's probably the coolest thing that could ever happen in a toilet (which isn't saying much) and the good news is, I'm going to tell you exactly what happens to me.

If I were you, I'd listen really carefully because no one is ever again going to tell you what it's like being flushed down a toilet, ever. Bear in mind I share the experience of being flushed away with **poo, wee** and **dead goldfish,** none of which are any good at story telling. If I had to choose which one I'd prefer to tell me about their flushing experience I'd probably go for the goldfish but then, well, it's dead so I may as well pick the poo or the wee.

Anyway, the only person that will ever tell you what it's really like is me, so listen up.

As soon as I press the flush, freezing cold water rushes in and soaks my legs. This is the most **unpleasant** part and I shiver as the icy flow covers my feet. I take a deep breath and slowly count to three. One, two, three. I start to turn around and round. Picking up speed with every turn. In a few seconds I'm spinning faster and **faster**. Everything is a blur,

I can't focus on anything. Round and round, spinning, spinning, faster and faster until I'm **whizzing** round at 150 miles per hour and then –

# WHOOOSH!

– there is a loud sucking noise in my ears and I get pulled straight down the toilet. Getting round the **U-bend** is a bit uncomfortable but the pressure of the water makes it happen in less than two seconds and then I'm on the biggest, fastest, craziest water slide you could ever imagine!

Go on, imagine the longest, fastest most exciting water chute in the world. Trust me, you **aren't even close**. This one is way, way, way longer, faster and more exciting.

I am almost deafened by the **roar** of

the fast-flowing water carrying me off
back in time. All I can see either side of me
are little flickers of light. It's like travelling
into space, but it's not black, it's all
different colours – reds, greens, blues,
purples – they all swirl and mix and blend
into one long tunnel of bright colour. I slide
faster and faster, it gets more difficult to
tell one colour from another. The slide takes
me on two huge *loop-the-loops* that
make my stomach feel funny. The force
of the twists and turns have made me pick
up speed again, I must be travelling at 300
miles per hour. Then I start turning down
and round, like being on a helter-skelter.

Faster and FASTER I turn round
and round further and further down and
then the slide suddenly vanishes beneath
me, the ride comes to an end and I float into

nothing as if being carried by a cloud. It's **completely** silent as if someone has pressed the mute button on a television. From then on, I just float around in a kind of **BUBBLE.** It's very quiet and very relaxing. All I have to do is sit tight and wait until I've travelled back far enough. Sometimes it feels like it takes forever, sometimes it's really quick, but I don't mind, as this part of the journey is so peaceful. I forget about school and indecisive parents and *Chloe* Onions. Yes, *EVEN* Chloe Onions!

I close my eyes and smile. Travelling back to **ROMAN** times would mean I'm heading back to approximately 55 BC. By my calculations I think that I'll arrive just about... **now.**

## CHAPTER 6

The sound of over 30,000 soldiers marching
could be heard from miles around. It sounded
just like the steady beat of a drum as they
marched in perfect formation. It was an
*incredible* sight; everyone was dressed
in deep red tunics with gleaming gold
breastplates and shiny gold helmets. There
were **noisy chariots** rattling on
the uneven ground. Large, muscular horses
pulled these beautiful gold chariots. Some of
the soldiers held a dangerous looking sword;

others carried a long, scary-looking **spear**.

(I later found out that a year earlier, **12,000** soldiers had planned to land in Dover but the BRITONS were ready for them and fought them off. With the army covering the beach, the **ROMANS** were forced to fight in the sea, which left them frightened, slow and cross about having to run about in wet sandals.)

Now, they had returned in greater numbers, armed with spears and swords and wearing those little blue overshoes that you get at swimming pools. (Ha! Not really - I'm *joking!*)

Some soldiers rode huge horses covered in armour. They looked magnificent as they effortlessly pulled golden chariots packed with only the best warriors. The **deaf-ening** noise of the chariot wheels sounded like thunder. It was an awesome sight designed to strike fear into the hearts of anyone that saw them. Except for one young boy who had just suddenly appeared in their path. That young boy was me.

'**HALT!**' shouted the man at the front, raising his hand. Immediately it fell silent as thousands of feet instantly stopped moving. The horses whinnied *ANGRILY* as they too were forced to stop. They shook their heads with annoyance causing big blobs of **horse dribble** to fly from their mouths and cover all the soldiers that were unlucky enough to be standing nearby. The soldiers stayed perfectly still. They were far too professional and well trained to make a fuss, even with horse dribble dripping off their noses.

Beyond the first two rows of soldiers, no one could see the reason that they were suddenly forced to stop. They just waited obediently to be told what to do next. It was an amazing sight. I desperately wanted to jump up and shout a command at them. I had so many great ideas but I was too scared to say any of them. Here are my ideas and why I didn't attempt to get the thousands of soldiers to do them:

**Fantastic idea #1:** Play a huge game of Simon Says.

**The reason I didn't do it:** All the soldiers were carrying sharp spears and if I shouted, 'Simon Says put your hands on your head', I was worried that at least half of them would end up being poked up the nose with the pointy bit.

**Fantastic idea #2:** Take a massive selfie of the soldiers and me.

**The reason I didn't do it:** Cameras weren't invented until 1816, and mobile phone cameras weren't invented until 2002. I have arrived in 55 B.C. (Before Cameras ... I think) and the only possible way I could get a selfie was to hire an artist to paint a picture. Getting 30,000 soldiers to stand still and smile while someone painted us would take far too long.

**Fantastic idea #3:** Get everybody dancing to a tune I play with armpit farts.

**The reason I didn't do it:** Don't get me wrong, there is nothing, and I mean NOTHING, funnier than making fart noises with your armpit. However, these soldiers did not look ready for that level of comedy performance.

What *actually* happened was that I stayed quiet and just admired how well behaved they all were. I'd never seen so many people do as they are told so quickly. In my school 30 children struggle to walk 100 yards from the classroom to the school hall in single file without fighting, ARGUING or throwing school bags at each other!

So, there I was face-to-face-to-face-

to-face-to-face (x 30,000) with all these
soldiers all waiting to find out who I was and
why I was interrupting their invasion. They
looked **pretty cross** and I thought
that at this exact moment, asking them if
they wouldn't all mind helping me with my
school project was not going to go down
particularly well. I was in LONDON
but it looked very different to how it looks
nowadays. I looked around and noticed
how empty it was. There were no high-rise
buildings or office blocks or shops. In fact,
there weren't any landmarks at all. There
were just endless fields and barren
land with long dirt tracks that created the
path that the soldiers were marching along.
Well, they **were** marching along until I
got in the way and now that they had been
interrupted they *did not* look very pleased.

# CHAPTER 7

A **large** man stared down at me and stroked his chin. (Just to clarify, he stroked his *own* chin, *I* didn't stroke his chin. Although, it would've been really funny to do so – you know, just give it a little stroke as he bent down. It would've also been really weird.)

His shiny metal helmet and chest plate glistened in the sun making me *squint* from the reflection.

'What is your name?' he bellowed.

I took a deep breath and nervously told him my name was Terry Barry Larry Gary Harry Jerry Perry Lenny Benny Johnny Tommy Julie Jones. He looked confused and after a long pause said, 'You have many, many names. Some would even say that you have *too* many. I shall just call you Julius.'

'Actually, I need to tell you... ' I started to explain that one of my names was Julie rather than Julius, but he interrupted me by raising his hand.

'**JULIUS** is a strong name, a leader's name. Now, what were you saying?'

I preferred what he was saying rather than what I was saying so decided not to continue telling him what I had started saying.

'I was just saying that I need to tell you that... I... umm... agree with you about my name being all strong and leader-y.'

'Hang on, you can't agree with something I say before I say it.'

'Yes I can,' I argued.

'But I hadn't said it yet.'

'Yes you did,' I continued to argue.

'When?'

'Just then.'

'You can only agree with me <u>after</u> I've said it. Not *before*.'

'I agree,' I agreed.

He gave me another confused look, which was only fair, as I hadn't a clue what I was talking about. I was just relieved that I was having a conversation and not being poked with a sword. I decided to win him over with my best smile.

'Why are you smiling in that strange way?'

I didn't know.

'I don't know,' I said.

'You are a strange boy. You have held us up for too long. We must continue our invasion. **Stand aside!'** he shouted, waving his hand to indicate that I should stand aside.

'Invade?' I asked 'What are you invading?'

'Londinium. We have travelled from Rome in Italy. We are the Roman army. The finest army in the world.'

'Italy? I *love* pizza,' I said rubbing my stomach hungrily.

'What is pizza?'

Oops, I forgot I was visiting 55 BC. Pizza hasn't been invented yet. In fact, it wasn't invented until 1889.

'It's a type of food. A base of dough with cheese, tomatoes and other toppings.'

'Sounds interesting, young Julius. I like

64

the sound of this pizza. Perhaps we shall prepare one and name it after our great leader, **CAESAR.**'

'He sounds more like a salad to me,' I offered. The solider looked confused and a little bit annoyed so I quickly asked him another question.

'What do you Romans like to eat, then?'

'Hare.'

'**Yuck!** I had one of them in my soup once. I did not carry on eating it.'

'I said hare, not hair!'

Now it was my turn to look confused. He sighed.

'A hare is like a wild rabbit,' he explained.

'**Double yuck.** I wouldn't like to be invited to dinner with you!' I said and folded my arms to show how much I meant it.

'That's good because I haven't invited you

65

to dinner, nor do I plan on making any dinner plans as I am in the middle of an invasion!' snapped the man, folding his arms.

We stood for a while, both **REFUSING** to look at each other. He eventually broke the silence.

'I SUPPOSE you could join us for something to eat later,' he sighed. 'We have fruit and nuts.'

'That sounds tastier. OK, I will.'

'But before we eat, you will join us and march with us. We do not rest and eat until sunset.'

I wasn't sure if I would like marching very much and I was totally sure I didn't want to join the Roman army but he had just invited me to dinner so it seemed a bit rude to argue. I stood up and brushed the dust off my clothes and then looked at the

**ROMAN** more closely.

'Can I ask you a question?' I asked, realising that by asking if I can ask him a question I'd already asked him a question, so even if he said 'no', it was too late, I'd already asked him one. Anyway, that wasn't the question I wanted to ask. It was a pre-question question.

'Be quick, we have a lot of ground to cover and it will be dark soon,' snapped the Roman.

'Umm... why are you wearing a skirt?' I asked.

**'What?'** shouted the man. A few of the other Roman soldiers laughed behind their hands. 'It is <u>NOT</u> a skirt,' he explained. 'It is a very smart tunic.'

'Skirt,' I corrected.

'Tunic,' he argued.

'Skirt,' I argued back. I know I said that

he invited me to dinner and I wasn't going to argue with him but he started it.

**– No he didn't.**

Now look here! You are the reader, you are not allowed to argue with me!

**– Yes I am.**

NO! NO! NO! This is <u>not</u> how books work. I write it and you read it. You don't get to argue important plot points with me midway through me telling a story.

**– It wasn't an important plot point. It was just a short piece of dialogue that you are using to develop some kind of relationship between you and a new character.**

STOP IT! You mustn't talk to me or I'll forget where I was. So, be quiet and let me finish the other argument that I was having with the Roman soldier.

Now, where was I?

**– Skirt.**

Sssh! Oh yes... thank you...

'Skirt,' I argued.

'**TUNIC!**' he shouted.

'Tunic – skirt, same thing to me,' I said.

'IT IS **NOT** THE SAME THING!' cried the man. 'All Roman men wear tunics made of wool, linen or silk.'

'Very **pretty,**' I said, giggling.

'I am not very pretty. I am a very strong, tough and mean Roman soldier!'

'True, but you are wearing a skirt,' I added, just as he produced a long spear and pointed the **sharp** bit an inch from my nose. I gulped.

'Umm... err... ' I stuttered. 'Did someone say skirt? How rude, it's clearly a *tunic*, made for men... umm... very big, strong, mean... soldiers who... umm look very tough and mean and strong when they wear them... ' I gave him my best smile and after a few minutes he lowered the spear.

'What are *you* wearing anyway?' he asked crossly.

'These?' I asked looking where he was pointing. 'They are trousers.'

'Trousers?' laughed the soldiers. 'No honourable man would wear trousers. Only grotty barbarians wear such a thing,' mocked the man. 'You are clearly a very confused young man.'

'What? You Romans are crazy!' I shouted just as the spear swung round and touched the tip of my nose again. 'Umm crazy... err... not to give me a tunic so I can get out of these grotty barbarian trousers.'

The soldier made a GROWLY noise from the back of his throat and ordered one of his men to find a spare tunic and give it to me. I wasn't too happy to change out of my comfortable trousers but it was preferable to having my nose prodded with a giant spear.

When I'd changed, I walked up and down getting used to my new outfit which, to my surprise, was actually quite comfortable. It was a bit breezy around the bottom area when the wind blew, but apart from that it wasn't too bad.

Why don't boys wear skirts for school? What if the ROMAN way was the same today and everyone wore skirts and only barbarians (i.e. teachers) wore trousers. No, it would be a bad idea. I once saw Maggie Marshall come out of the girls' toilet and her skirt was caught in her tights and everyone saw her underwear. I don't want anyone seeing my underwear. The pair I am wearing today have a **HOLE** in the... never mind. I think trousers might be the safer option for me.

I'm just wearing a tunic, OK. A boys' tunic. For *boys*! The kind of boys that have big holes in their boxer shorts. The kind of boys who need to go and buy new underwear. Yeah, that's me.

Anyway, you have big **HOLES** in your underwear. Yes you do, how do you get your legs in then? Haha! I'm part of the **ROMAN** army and yet still have time to tell an amazing joke. Feel free to share that joke with all your friends.

What do you mean, **no?**

# CHAPTER 8

The marching was really tiring and I quickly dropped back. I was soon **huffing** and **puffing** trying to keep up with some of the other soldiers.

'Roman men don't only wear tunics,' whispered one young soldier. 'If you are rich, you get to wear a toga.'

'You mean like a huge wild big cat with the sharp claws and the—'

'No, that's a tiger,' interrupted the soldier. 'I said **toga**.'

'Oh. What's a toga?' I asked.

'It is a long robe draped around the body. It's very smart,' he said proudly.

'Well, it's better than wearing a tiger,' I commented.

'Nobody wears tigers.' He shook his head and sighed.

I thought about what he was describing. 'A toga sounds similar to a dressing gown,' I said.

'What is a dressing gown? I have never heard of such a thing.'

'It's a type of robe. You put it on when you get out of the bath.'

'Ahh, now you are talking sense. A ROMAN bath is the best place to join your friends and relax.'

'You have a bath with your friends?' I asked with a shocked look on my face.

'Of course, don't you?'

'Well, I had a bath with my cousin when we were much younger but then one day she did a **wee** and that was it. I am not staying in a bath that she has had a wee in...'

'Your cousin? Now that is strange. Roman baths are **magnificent** buildings where we go to meet friends, relax and wash. Some of the grander bathhouses even have restaurants and libraries in them. They are wonderful places.' Some of the other soldiers who were listening nodded in agreement.

'Libraries? But don't the books get all **soggy?**' I asked. The soldiers all looked at me with confused faces.

'You don't know much do you, Julius?'

'Not really, but I'm learning lots, and I love relaxing in a hot bath.'

'Ahh, but what about the tepidarium?'

'The what?'

'A tepidarium is a cold bath to ease tired muscles. Have you never had a Cold bath?'

'Well, once when our central heating broke down.' I nodded.

'Ahh, heating, invented by us.'

'You?'

'Well, not me exactly but by the ROMANS. We invented heating, baths, straight roads...'

'The English language,' shouted another soldier who was standing behind us.

'Of course! We invented the English language, which is based on LATIN, which is the language we normally speak to each other. I don't suppose you speak Latin, do you?'

'Nope. I don't even know what a Latin is,

to be honest.'

The soldiers looked at me and sighed.

'So, why aren't you talking in Latin now?' I asked.

'Well, you know the old saying – when in BRITAIN!' A few of the other soldiers laughed loudly at this comment. I had no idea what he was talking about but didn't want to let on, so I too laughed loudly. A little too loudly in fact and they all stopped and stared at me.

'Well, I invented a water slide that goes from my bedroom window through my tree house, round the shed and then into the paddling pool in my garden. Well, when I say invented I mean I drew it on a piece of paper, but it was technically brilliant and would definitely have worked.' I was waving my arms around getting overexcited and when I looked up all the soldiers were staring at me.

'What's a tree house?' said one.

'What's a paddling pool?' asked another.

'What's a banana milkshake?' said the third man.

'Banana milkshake? I never mentioned a banana milkshake. Who mentioned banana milkshakes? How do you know about them?' I asked.

'About what?' stuttered the soldier looking GUILTY.

'Banana milkshakes,' I said.

'Never heard of them,' he said, looking around. 'What's a banana milkshake then?'

I looked at him suspiciously. Could he be another TIME-TRAVELLER? Hmmm. I didn't get a chance to ask him because another soldier came over and was shouting about how we'd stopped marching. He started shouting commands in Latin.

'Sin, dex, sin, dex, sin, dex.' I worked out this meant left, right, left, right.

As we started to pick up the pace again, I joined in the commands but I kept getting my sin and my dex the wrong way round. Doing the Hokey Cokey must be a nightmare. I'd be putting my SIN leg in when I should be shaking my DEX leg all about. So anyway, to make things easier I went back to shouting in English.

We were marching along at quite an exhausting speed with me shouting commands. All the soldiers stepped in time. Left, right, left, right, left, right, left, left, left, right, right, right, right...

'Stop messing around, Julius. You are confusing the other soldiers!'

'Sorry!'

I fell back into the exhausting marching pace. It was so **boring,** I tapped the soldier next to me on the shoulder.

Ooh! A soldier's shoulder – that's a great tongue twister. Try saying it five times really fast!

What if one of the metal clips fell off his tunic and he had to solder it back on? He'd have to solder a soldier's shoulder.

What if he was a solder seller, selling solder to soldiers for their shoulders?

What if the solder seller started selling strollers and solder to the soldiers for their shoulder?

Well it wouldn't happen because even though solder was invented around 4000 BC to join two pieces of metal together, strollers weren't invented until 1733 to

carry the Duke of Devonshire's children.
So, the whole idea is ridiculous and
we should all just go back to the moment
I tapped the soldier on the shoulder. Ooh,
what if... I'm joking... carry on...

'What's your name?' I asked.

'CLAUDIUS,' he replied. 'Tiberius
Claudius Caesar Augustus Germanicus.'

'Haha. That's as silly as my name: Terry
Barry Larry Gary Harry Jerry Perry Lenny
Benny Johnny Tommy Julie Jones,' I laughed.

'I thought your name was JULIUS.'

'It is...'

'Are you sure?'

'Totally sure.'

'So, what was that name you just said?'

'What name?'

'The Barry, Carry, Marry, Flarry name?'

'No idea. Never heard of him.'

'And did you say <u>my</u> name was silly?'

'Nope.'

'Are you sure?'

'Yes, totally. If I have a boy one day, I'm definitely calling him **TIBERIUS CLAUDIUS CAESAR AUGUSTUS GERMANICUS.** It's the best name ever.'

'It will be declared the best name ever when I become Emperor of Rome. You wait and see,' he whispered as he puffed out his chest and stuck his nose in the air pompously.

Actually, what he was telling me was true, CLAUDIUS became the Roman emperor from AD 41 to 54. He, too, tried to conquer Britain. If there is one thing that I am learning about Roman emperors, it's that they all really want to get their hands on Britain. If I was a Roman emperor I'd tell everyone to give up their swords and shields and have a massive **party** and people would bring me really nice presents and I wouldn't even have to write them a thank-you card because I'd make it the law that emperors didn't have to write thank-you cards.

I looked over at Claudius and he was still standing with his nose in the air dreaming of becoming emperor. I tapped him on the shoulder again.

'What else did the Romans invent?' I whispered. He thought about it for a few moments and then said, 'One of our greatest inventions is the calendar. Our great ruler, JULIUS CAESAR, invented it. He studied the movement of the earth around the sun and then created the solar calendar with 365 days a year. Did you know that some of the months are named after Roman gods and rulers?'

'No, **I didn't know that,** I said.

'You don't know much, do you, Julius?'

'You've said that before. You don't need to keep telling me how much I don't know. It's very **RUDE.** Maybe if you are going to say something negative you should finish by saying something positive too. Like, "You don't know much, Julius, but you have *lovely* hair".'

'But I don't like your hair,' he said.

'What's wrong with my hair?'

'Nothing really. I just don't like it,' he shrugged.

I marched along silently for a few minutes wondering what exactly was wrong with my hair.

Eventually, the soldier next to me spoke.

'Our great emperor Julius Caesar had
a month named after him. Surely you can
guess which month is named after Julius?'

'March?' I guessed based on the fact
that from what I've seen, they did seem to
do quite a lot of marching – so it sounded
sensible to me.

'No. March is the first month and is named
after Mars, the god of war.'

'Wait a minute. Did you just say
that March is the first month?'

'Yes, of course. You don't know anything,
do you? March is the first month, April is
named after the Latin word 'to open', and
May was named after Maia, the earth
goddess of growing plants.'

April and May – springtime, I thought.
Makes sense.

The soldier continued, 'June is the most

popular month to get married so it's named after the gods of marriage and weddings. August is named after Augustus Caesar, the first emperor of **THE ROMAN EMPIRE.** September, October, November and December are from the LATIN words Septem, Octo, Novem and Decem which are Latin for seven, eight, nine and ten.

'Which would make sense if it weren't for the fact that March isn't the first month,' I said.

'What?' asked the soldier.

'Nothing, carry on,' I smiled.

'That's it.'

'What?'

'That's all the nine months. You really need to pay attention in school.'

**QUICK NOTE:** I looked this up when I

got home and he was right.

February was added in around 690 BC at the end of the year and was a period of celebration. It was a festival called Februa. Finally, January was added at the beginning of the year. It's named after Janus, the god of beginnings and endings.

It wasn't until 1583 that a pope called Gregory changed the order — the same one we follow today — then it was called the Gregorian calendar. By then I guess it was too late to change the names of the months. It would be like me suddenly telling everyone that I was rearranging the days of the week. To Wednesday, Monday, Tuesday afternoon, Thursday, Friday night, Tuesday morning, Saturday, Sunday and then Friday morning. Actually, if I could change the days of the week I'd change them to Saturday, Sunday, Saturday, Sunday, Saturday, Sunday and Saturday.

'So, back to my question. What month is named after Julius?'

'November,' I laughed. 'I'm joking, it's July, July is named after Julius Caesar.'

'Of course,' answered the soldier.

'See, I **DO** know something,' I grinned, feeling pleased with myself.

'Very good, Julius, you are learning,' the man smiled. We were getting on great, so I thought I'd ask one more thing.

'Can I have a toga to wear?' I smiled.

He suddenly stopped marching, causing three soldiers behind him to bash into each other.

'Are you a rich **ROMAN** citizen?'

'Ummm... what would you say if I said yes?' I asked.

'I'd say of course you should have a toga.'

'Then... yes!' I said hopefully.

'Fetch Julius a toga!' he shouted to another soldier, who immediately rushed around searching one of the chariots until he'd found one. They showed me the toga, I nodded my approval, draped it around my shoulders and tied the middle with a belt made of rope. I did look very smart and it was very easy to march in, although I still wasn't sure about the breeze around my **bottom.**

# CHAPTER 9

I marched for a little while, trying to keep up. I had no idea how **boring** marching was. I tried really hard to concentrate, but I would only be in 55 BC for a short time and I had to learn as much as possible, which meant asking as many questions as I could. I started with what I considered to be an important one.

'Why are you invading BRITAIN?'

'We are looking for riches,' explained one of the soldiers. 'Iron, lead, zinc, copper, silver and gold and, of course, land and slaves. All these things will make us rich men.'

'That's quite a shopping list.' I nodded thoughtfully. 'I don't think they sell any of those things in the supermarket, you'd probably be better off going to a DIY store.'

'A what?'

'Nothing,' I said, and quickly changed the subject. 'Hey, what do you call a man in a boat with a paddle?'

'I do not know,' said the soldier. 'What do you call a man in a boat with a paddle?'

'A **ROW-MAN,**' I laughed.

'I did not know that,' said the man seriously.

'No, it's a joke. Row-man sounds like Roman. It's a play on words.' I tried to explain but the men were looking at each other and scratching their heads.

91

'We have no time to play, we must march and then fight,' he snapped and then we all continued marching in silence.

I don't like not talking so I turned to the soldier behind me and asked him if he liked his schooldays.

'My teacher was very **STRICT.** She believed that young people should not be playing when they are learning. But she taught me to speak, write, tell the time and count money. I also learned public speaking.'

'That doesn't sound much fun,' I shrugged.

**'Fun?** Learning is not considered a reason to have fun. Education is taken very seriously. You, young man, are too busy having fun and that's why you will never go far.'

'I've come further than you think,' I snapped. Romans were so **RUDE.**

'We think you are a very strange young man.' He was a thin nasty-looking soldier who had been staring at me earlier. 'You talk about strange things like Row Mans—'

'That was a joke,' I interrupted.

'And jokes, whatever they are. You don't speak like a **ROMAN** or dress like one.'

'Well that's where you are wrong because look, I'm wearing a tiger.' I corrected him nervously.

'Toga,' whispered the man next to me.

'That's what I said,' I whispered back.

'**No**, you said you were wearing a tiger.'

'Why would I say that? Tigers are big cats, you can't wear them.'

'**I KNOW THAT!**' snapped the man in the loudest whisper possible, before it stops becoming a whisper and turns into a shout.

'Be silent,' hissed the skinny soldier. 'I do not believe that you are a Roman soldier or a rich Roman citizen. I think you are an imposter. I have a feeling that you might even be a BRITON!'

A few of the soldiers that were close by gasped. I tried my best not to look guilty, but I knew that whenever I tried not to look guilty I looked even **GUILTIER.** I couldn't help it. Like when my mum asked, 'Who painted green stripes on your trousers?' and I felt really guilty even though... oh, no wait, that was me. I was quite right to feel guilty.

The suspicious soldier interrupted my train of thought by shouting at me again. 'If I find out that you are a Briton then you will become our slave.' The corners of his mouth turned up slightly in a cruel sneer.

'Oh, I don't think I'd be a very good slave.

I once tried to do some ironing and burned a big hole in Mum's best shirt. She was <u>not</u> happy with me.'

'**SILENCE!**' shouted the man. 'Seize the imposter! Chain him up with the rest of the slaves we have captured.'

'Now **wait a minute**, I was just...'

The soldier put his face very close to mine, perhaps a little too close as our noses were almost touching. If I'd have leaned forward a tiny bit, I could've quite easily *kissed* the end of his nose. Although, I should point out that I had **no intention** of kissing his nose. In fact, I was scared – really scared (not of his nose – I was scared of all of him). I did not want to end up becoming a slave. I could feel the heat of his breath on my face. It smelled of how you'd imagine a man would **smell** who does nothing but march along all day occasionally eating dried fruit and hairs.

He stared at me without blinking.

I closed my eyes really tightly, held my breath for three seconds, quickly raised my right arm and pumped it up and down really fast. Finally, I repeated the word 'home' over and over again. Just as I heard him shout, **'Seize** him now! **Lock him up!'** I squeezed my eyes shut extra tightly, crossed my fingers and hoped more than I'd ever hoped before that I'd head back to the present day.

## CHAPTER 10

A few moments later, I **nervously** opened one eye, then the other one and was relieved to see that I was back in my **toilet** at home. For some reason, the journey coming back to the present takes only a few seconds. There is no **water slide** or drifting around floating on clouds, it just sort of happens. One minute I'm there and the next minute I'm back here. I don't know why. But then I don't know why, when I stand in my toilet, I can **TRAVEL BACK**

**IN TIME.** As I said, it just sort of happens.

I breathed a sigh of relief. I have never been so happy to see my toilet. (Actually, there was the time that I ate a dodgy fishcake for my school dinner and had to run home really fast. On that occasion I was **relieved** to see my toilet for a whole other reason that I do not want to go into right now – or ever!)

I dried my feet and put my socks back on. I was just about to unlock the door and leave the bathroom when I caught sight of myself in the mirror. I gasped in surprise. I was still wearing the toga. What a perfect way to present my project at school, dressed in traditional **ROMAN** clothes. I'd look so strong and brave and handsome that Chloe couldn't help but notice me. I opened the bathroom door and bumped straight into my mum.

'Where on **earth** have you been?' she asked.

'Rome,' I said.

'What?' she snapped.

'Err... home... I've been at home,' I stumbled.

'And what on earth are you wearing?' she cried.

'I am wearing a toga. It's for my school project on the Romans. I thought I'd dress up.' Mum looked me up and down suspiciously.

'I hope you **HAVEN'T** made that out of one of my good bed sheets?' she asked.

'No.'

'Where did you get it from then?'

'Erm... I just kind of made it with bits and pieces I found,' I lied.

'Well, it looks very well made.'

99

'Thank you,' I said proudly.

Mum stood with her hands on her hips eyeing me *suspiciously.*

I returned to my bedroom and closed the door. I found my project book under a pile of books and started to write. I have a whole week to produce an **amazing** project. I wrote down everything that I remembered and learned from the soldiers. I wrote about all the inventions that had come from the ROMANS and as many details of the invasion as I could recall. Over the next few days, I drew fantastic pictures with lots of detail. I stayed in my room and worked for hours and hours.

Eventually, Mum came in and said that she was pleased I was working so hard on my homework but that I needed to go out and get some fresh air as my bedroom was starting to **smell.**

'Rude,' I muttered under my breath.

'Well, why don't you go and see Ollie?'

'Good idea,' I agreed.

'... Or maybe one of your other friends like...'

'**NO, MUM!** Stop. A decision has been made, no need to complicate it. I am going to see Ollie,' I quickly said before Mum got into one of her weird indecisive moments.

I grabbed my coat, shouted **good-bye** to mum and left the house. Ollie only lived in the next road so it only took a few minutes before I was ringing on his doorbell. I kept my finger on it until he answered.

Dingdongdingdong!

Ollie eventually opened the door.

'**Shhhh,** my dad's trying to sleep,' he whispered.

I kept leaning on the doorbell and shouted back, 'WHAT? I can't hear you when you whisper and your doorbell keeps ringing. Speak up, Ollie. What did you say?'

Dingdongdingdong!

'I SAID STOP RINGING THE DOORBELL!' shouted Ollie at the top of his voice.

'STOP SHOUTING, OLLIE! I'm trying to get to SLEEP!' shouted his dad, sounding very cross.

'Now look what you've done! I'm in trouble now!' groaned Ollie.

'Well, you should get your doorbell fixed,' I laughed, pushing past him and taking my coat off.

'How's your project coming along?' I asked him when we were sitting in his bedroom.

'Good. In fact, really good. I think I could win the prize. I've been working all week to create something really special. There are famous quotes, reviews of films about the subject and I've even written my own poem,' he bragged.

'A poem? Really? Read it to me,' I asked suspiciously.

'No way.'

'Go on.'

'You'll laugh.'

'No, I won't.'

'Promise?'

'Of course.'

'OK then.' Ollie reached over to his desk and grabbed an A4 folder. He opened it up and flicked through a few pages until he found the one he was looking for.

'Check this out,' he smiled.

'I love her more than words could say,

I love her in a very special way,

I love her like I love spaghetti,

and I look at her more than I watch the telly.

I love the way she—'

'WOAH, WOAH, WOAH! What on earth are you reading me here, Ollie?' I asked, scratching my head in confusion.

'It's my project. Cool, huh? No one else will think of writing a love poem.'

'A *love* poem? Why have you written a love poem? You do realise that we are supposed to be doing a project about the ROMANS?'

'*Romans*? I thought it was supposed to be about romance! Oh, no! I've just spent four days drawing love hearts and writing soppy poems. I even painted the front cover pink. PINK! Romans don't wear pink? Or do they? Maybe they do! They don't, do they? Agghhhh! What am I going to do?'

'Tell the class that you are really in love with the Romans?'

'You are not being helpful! I have two days to do a whole project. I'll stand **NO** chance of winning the prize!' wailed Ollie.

'You didn't stand a chance anyway because I am going to win it,' I boasted.

'Arrgghh! You have to go home now, I have a lot of work to do,' shouted Ollie pushing me out of his bedroom, down the stairs and out the front door.

'Oh, wait,' I called back just as he was shoving me out of his house. He stopped pushing me for a moment. 'Do me a favour. When I win the prize and Chloe falls in love with me, can I borrow your poem?' I asked, trying not to laugh.

'*AARRRGGGHH!*' he shouted, slamming the door.

'Bye!' I shouted through the letterbox. 'I love you more than spaghetti and telly!' I could just about hear his dad bellowing that he was still trying to get to sleep as I walked back home giggling to myself all the way.

I was proud of the work I'd done, all thanks to my **TIME-TRAVELLING** toilet. All I needed to do now was to get some well-deserved rest and then wake up for school in two days' time feeling refreshed and ready to hand in my MASTERPIECE. All that then remained was for me to receive top marks and win the heart of the girl of my dreams. What could possibly go wrong...?

# CHAPTER 11

Mr Munford stood on the school stage and looked out at all the 350 pupils of Stage Mount High. I stood next to him. When he had absolute silence, he began to speak.

'The winner of the greatest project **EVER** written about the Romans goes to **Ted Jones.** He has proved himself to be a true genius. Please accept this prize of £1 million, this top-of-the-range computer, a new bike, another computer and our promise that you will never be given a detention ever again. As a special surprise you will also become the youngest person ever to receive the Nobel Peace Prize and be knighted by the Queen of England. It is an honour to have you as a pupil.' Mr Munford sobbed with joy as he shook my hand. Everyone started cheering and clapping.

# TED JONES! TED JONES! TED JONES!

'TED JONES! Will you wake up! You've overslept and if you don't hurry, you'll be late for school!'

I opened my eyes to see my mother standing over me with her hands on her hips. I turned my head to look at my clock. 08:15. That gives me *exactly* fifteen minutes to:

**Get washed** (I could leave this out, I smell OK... ish)

**Get dressed** (I can't leave this out, it's

important for school)

**Eat breakfast** (I could leave this out, but don't want to)

**Get to school** (No time to wait for Mum to make a decision about what driving shoes to wear or if she needs to take an umbrella. I had to move quickly and if Mum was to get me to school on time I would have to make all the decisions for her)

'MUM!' I called 'There's no time for breakfast I'll just take a banana, wear your black driving shoes, your long coat, no need for an umbrella, your hair looks fine, you don't need to put on any make-up, the windows are all locked, the quickest way to get there is straight up the high street. If we **HURRY** we can make it!'

Mum stood at the bottom of the stairs looking stunned.

'Right then,' she said. 'Let's go, we've got twelve minutes before the gate shuts.'

I hastily put on my toga, picked up the box with my project in and ran for the door. As I ran out of the house, my next-door neighbour Mr Ringle was also coming out of his house. He waved to me.

'That's a *lovely* dress you're wearing, Ted. Is it new?' he asked.

'It's not a dress, Mr Ringle. It's a toga.'

He did reply, but I didn't hear him as I was already in the car with the door shut.

'Go! Go! Go! Step on it! Hurry! *HURRY!* I can't be late today.'

'OK, OK,' said Mum. 'This isn't an episode of *Starsky and Hutch*, you know?'

'I'm too young to know or understand what you just said,' I replied.

'Really? What about *The Dukes of*

*Hazard*?'

'Nope, no idea.'

'*Miami Vice*?'

'Never heard of it.'

**Really?** Oh dear... what about—'

I interrupted her. 'Mum, concentrate on getting me to school on time. We will talk about random programmes from the 1970s later. If you get me there on time, I'll even sit and watch one with you after school.'

'Really?' said mum sounding excited.

**'No way!'** I replied.


Fortunately, the only other school in the area went back a day after my school, so traffic was lighter than usual, and Mum's car pulled up at the school gates with three minutes to spare. Mr Munford was standing at the gate as usual.

'Why are you wearing a dress, Mr Jones?' he asked the moment I got out of the car.

'It's a toga, sir,' I said. 'As part of my project I thought I'd come in traditional dress.'

'I see,' said Mr Munford thoughtfully. 'And where did you get the toga?'

**'ANCIENT ROME,'** I said honestly.

'Don't be cheeky, young man!' he snapped back.

I started to walk off, towards my lesson. Mr Munford called after me.

'Jones!' he shouted. 'Good effort, boy. I'll be sure to give you extra points for the costume.'

'Thanks, sir! You're all right,' I smiled.

'Am I indeed? Now tell me, at what point did you plan to change back into your school uniform?' he asked.

'Ummm… I thought I'd… ' I was trying to come up with an excuse as to why I'd forgotten to bring in my school uniform, when Ollie ran up behind me and nearly knocked me over in the scramble to get through the gates. He was carrying a folder with a few pages of work. He didn't look happy.

'You're a very lucky boy. The gate should've closed two minutes ago. As long as your project is a masterpiece, I will allow you to enter,' he said.

'Thanks, sir,' gulped Ollie looking guiltily at his painted pink folder. The headmaster eyed the folder with suspicion.

'I must admit, it doesn't look as extensive as the box that Ted is carrying.'

'No, sir, but at least I didn't come to school

in a **dress,**' he joked.

'It's a toga,' I corrected.

'We all know what it is!' snapped the head teacher immediately going back to being his usual grumpy self. 'Put the projects in the hall with the others and make your way to class. Judging will begin at first break.'

Ollie and I walked across the playground towards the hall.

'So, why are you wearing a dress?' he whispered.

'It's a toga. Anyway, in ancient Rome trousers were considered uncivilised,' I sighed.

'Well it's a good job we aren't in ancient Rome then, isn't it?' said Ollie.

Something told me that despite all my great work, today wasn't going to go as well as I'd imagined.

# CHAPTER 12

My day did **not** go as well as I'd imagined. Here is how my morning went...

> **Everyone I saw:** 'Hi, Ted. Why are you wearing a dress?'
> **Me (to everyone I saw):** 'It's a toga.'

By lunchtime I was regretting ever wearing a toga. I just thought it would help me win the competition (and the heart of my beloved *Chloe*).

By the end of lunch break, we still hadn't had any news from the judges. It was when we were in the middle of **double Maths** that a message came round from the headmaster that, due to the amount and quality of the projects, judging would take another day. ＡＮＯＴＨＥＲ ＤＡＹ! By then everyone would've forgotten what I'd been through whilst wearing a toga. The plan was that I was supposed to collect my winner's prize in full costume. Tomorrow was no good – I'd be back in school uniform. I'd either have to wear the toga again (not going to happen) or bring it with me and get changed (too early and I'd look too confident, too late and there wouldn't be any time). What a fashion **DISASTER!** As I silently cursed my bad luck, I heard voices behind me.

'Nice dress!' they giggled. I was just about to turn around and shout that it was a toga, but when I turned I was face-to-face with Chloe (hooray) and Sandra (Booo).

'Why are, like, you, like wearing a dress? I'm like so going to tell the teacher,' said Sandra.

I ignored her and looked at Chloe. The shocking thing is that she was looking at me, and noticing me, and talking to me! I couldn't believe it!

'It suits you... I think,' laughed Chloe.

'Yeah, thanks.' I smiled, blushing bright red. **'HA HA, YOU'RE WEARING A DRESS!'** shouted Martin Harris, the class bully.

'No, I'm *not*! It's a **toga**.'

'But, you just said it was a dress. Which

means you are wearing a dress.' He sneered and pointed at my face. 'Ted's wearing a dress! Ted's wearing a dress!' he sang, taunting me further. I chose to ignore him and turned back to continue to talking to Chloe and... she'd gone!

NOOOOOOOOOOOO!!!

Martin Harris had ruined every-thing! I was so angry I spun back to face the bully.

'**ACTUALLY,** in Roman times the important men wore the togas and only **GROTTY** people wore trousers. They were the lowest of the low. Even men that weren't important wore tunics. However, *you*, Martin Harris, would be lucky to have a **potato sack** to wear. Yes, that's right, a sack that you put potatoes in! But you'd know all of that if you'd studied the

**ROMANS** and produced a decent project. And, for the record, if we lived in Roman times and **you** had nothing to wear, and **I** had a potato sack, I would rather keep potatoes in it than give it to you – **and I don't even like potatoes!** (Except chips. I really like chips!)

I'd finished my *RANT* and I stared at Martin. I was breathing heavily and my face was red. The whole classroom was completely silent. You could've heard a pin drop.

**DING**!

Someone dropped a pin. (I heard it. Told you.)

Martin pointed at me and looked like he was about to say something, but nothing came out. He just waggled his finger up and down, let out a little squeak and then went and sat at the back of the classroom to sulk.

Suddenly, a huge noise **ERUPTED.**
Everyone started to cheer my name.
Classmates were high-fiving me. I'd stood up
to the bully and won, I was a hero! I looked
around the class and there she was – the
most beautiful onion in the world. Actually,
that doesn't sound right. Let me write that
bit again...

... I looked around the class and there she
was – the most *beautiful* girl in the
world – Chloe Onions. And she was smiling at
me!

That's better.

I smiled back and turned a little bit red.
She walked over to me and was just about
to speak when her best friend Sandra Wum
(AKA **Sandy Bum**) appeared.

'Hi, Chloe, I've, like, got a cool new album

on my phone. Come and listen to it,' she said, pulling on Chloe's arm.

Sandra was one of the only pupils to have her own phone. I think it made her more popular. Not with me it didn't.

But then something **amazing** happened. Chloe pushed Sandra's arm away and said, 'No, you go ahead. I want to speak to Ted.'

Did you hear that? She **wants** to speak to me! She could choose to do anything in the world right now but instead she actually **WANTS** to speak to me!

'I think your toga makes you look cool,' she said, smiling.

Did you hear that? She actually said – OK, I'm going to stop repeating everything she said. I think you understand by now that I

was surprised and excited by this
conversation.

'Thanks,' I said.

'Where did you get it?'

'Ancient Rome,' I replied honestly.

'You're funny,' she giggled.

**DID YOU HEAR THAT?**

She said I was... sorry, sorry,
I forgot... no repeating things.
Sorry... carry on...

'Thanks,' I said.

'We should **HANG OUT** sometime,
we could go to the cinema or something.'

'I'd like that,' I smiled. 'I could wear my
toga, if you want?'

'No, **DON'T DO THAT,**' she laughed.

'No,' I agreed. 'I think I might go back to
normal clothes from now on.'

I didn't want to bring this conversation to

**122**

an end, but at that moment our teacher, Miss Makeshift, walked into class and told us all to sit down and open our workbooks. **Work?** How was I expected to do any work? I had just handed in a (hopefully) award-winning project and the prettiest girl in the school was having a proper conversation with me.

'Sigh, I am in *love*.'

'You just said that out loud,' whispered Ollie nudging me in the ribs.

'What?'

'You just said that you were in love, out loud and now everyone is looking at you.' Ollie shrugged. 'I just thought you should know.'

I looked around and sure enough the whole class was now looking at me.

All of them were laughing.

Groan.

# CHAPTER 13

'Right, **settle down!**' Mr Munford shouted, clapping his hands together to signal the start of our school assembly the following morning. A couple of the more enthusiastic teachers made shushing noises, spraying the kids nearest to them with little droplets of saliva.

**Note to self:** Bring an umbrella to assembly in future. Just in case.

When the hall had become silent, Mr Munford continued.

'Well done to you all on your **ROMAN** projects. The rest of the staff and I have read them all and we have been pleasantly surprised at how good they have been. You clearly enjoyed the topic, which we will be continuing throughout the term. We have decided to award **prizes** for the first, second and third places as well as a small prize to a runner-up.'

My heart started to pound a little faster. I didn't care about winning because I was way too cool for that – but at the same time I really, really, REALLY wanted to win. I mean, come on, the whole school may have looked up facts on the internet but I actually went to ancient Rome. How could I lose?

'Firstly, the runner-up, for creating his own version of **ROMAN** pottery, is William Peters,' announced the head. A few of William's friends clapped as a grinning boy went up and collected his prize. He proudly held up a brightly coloured clay blob.

'In third place, for a beautiful diorama showing a soldier and a chariot is Chloe Onions.'

Chloe stood and went up to collect her prize. I clapped extra hard, just so that she knew she had my full support.

'In second place, Ollie Wolf for his interesting and unusual look at romance during Roman times.'

What? Even Ollie looked confused. He was looking around to see if anyone else, with the same name, was going to stand up and collect the prize. He eventually stood up and walked onto the stage with a look of absolute surprise on his face. **How on earth** had he managed to get a prize for second place? When Mr Munford picked up the bright pink folder, Ollie quickly grabbed it and held it behind his back so that no one else saw it.

When the hall was quiet again, Mr Munford approached the microphone.

*This was it, my moment, come on...*

'And in first place ...'

*Yes?*

'... for a very detailed and accurate look at the Roman invasion of Britain ...'

*Yes? Yes... ?*

'... and for going that extra mile ...'

*YES? Get on with it!*

'... and coming to school in a remarkably authentic Roman toga ...'

# YES! YES! YES!

'... the prize goes to Ted Jones.'

YEEEEEESSSS! I'd done it! All
that work had paid off and there we were,
Chloe and I (and Ollie, but anyone who hands
in a project about the Romans in a folder
that has pink love hearts all over it doesn't
count in my book... oh, and William but who
cares about William and his blob pot?).

'Congratulations,' said Mr Munford as
I went up to shake his hand (yuck, all
sweaty) and accept my prize. The other
students and teachers clapped the four
of us.

Chloe leant over and whispered in my ear,
'Well done, Ted.'

'Thanks, you too,' I replied.

'Where did you get all your information
from?'

'The **toilet,**' I said knowingly. I was trying to come across as interesting and mysterious, rather than weird.

Chloe giggled. 'You're so weird,' she said.

Oh well, I guess I need more practice at being mysterious then. But, she was right, my life is a bit weird. I mean, come on, I can travel back in time via my toilet – I know that's not normal! But, who wants to be normal? Not me!

I leaned over to Chloe and whispered to her, 'I wish Mr Munford would stop talking. I need the toilet.'

'Will you find out more exciting things about ancient Rome in there?' she asked with a little giggle.

'Who knows? Maybe I will,' I replied. 'Who knows what secrets the toilet holds?'

As Mr Munford finished off the assembly with information about various after school clubs, Chloe turned to me and smiled. I leaned over to her again.

'I can tell you how the months got their names if you like?'

'No, thanks,' she replied and turned away.

The bell **rang** and the pupils started to file out and head out to the playground for break. Chloe was standing next to me and suddenly squealed with delight.

'I've just had a great idea!' she laughed.

'You do want me to teach you about how the months got their names?' I replied hopefully.

'No. Seriously, Ted, I never, ever want you to tell me that information.'

Strange, but fine, I'll respect her wishes.

'Ted, I've been invited to a **fancy-dress**

**party** this Saturday. The theme is ancient Roman. It's a toga party! You can come with me if you like?'

I gulped in surprise.

'I'd like that very much,' I **stumbled.**

'But you need to tell me where you got your toga. I've got to go and buy one as good as yours.'

'Ahh,' I said hesitantly. 'I'm... err... fairly sure the shop closed down.'

'Since yesterday?'

'Yeah, not a lot of call for togas round here really.'

Chloe laughed. 'You are SO silly, Ted. If I don't have a toga I can't go, and neither can you. So, you are going to have to help me get one.'

WoW, does Chloe have a bossy side? I know how to deal with that. I'll stand up to her, I thought to myself. I'll just say no to her. She will have to make one out of a bed sheet like everyone else will. There is no way I was going to be bossed around by her. I've stood up to **ROMAN** soldiers and I'm going to stand up to her. I looked her straight in the eye and said...

'Of course, I'll get you one. No problem at all. Leave it to me.'

Sigh. I was <u>rubbish</u> at this.

# CHAPTER 14

The moment I arrived back at my house, I **RAN** up the stairs taking two at a time. Mum called up the stairs after me.

'Hello, Ted, you're in a hurry. Is everything OK?'

'Yes, Mum,' I shouted back. 'I just really need the toilet.'

'Oh dear. What did you have for lunch?'

'Gravel and grass,' I said.

'Why on **earth** did you have that?' she asked sounding concerned.

'For a bet,' I said.

'A bet?' she shrieked 'What kind of bet?'

'I thought to myself, "I bet that tastes **revolting"**. I was right. It did.' I laughed. Mum just sighed and walked off shaking her head.

I ran into the bathroom and shut and locked the door. I couldn't believe I had to go back. I took off my shoes and socks and climbed into the toilet.

'Here we go again,' I said to myself.

I won't go through explaining the whole process again. I'll shorten the journey back in time for you. Basically, this happened:

*... Cold water. Deep breath. One, two, three. Twisting. Turning. Faster. Blurry vision. Whooshing. Ouch – round the U-Bend. Roaring noises. Flicky flicky lights. Lots of colours, lovely, lovely, red, green blue... Faster.*

*Loop-the-loops. Stomach funny. Going to throw up – no I'm not. Super-fast. Round and round. Floaty floaty... Shhhh silence. All relaxed. Nice and peaceful. Ahhh, all calm.*

**'Seize the imposter!** Chain him up with the rest of the slaves we have captured!'

Uh-oh!

I opened my eyes to see the soldier still in my face shouting. I was right back where I'd left off!

Right, don't panic, Ted. Let's just think carefully about my next move. All I had to do was convince 30,000 **ROMAN SOLDIERS** that I wasn't an imposter and was a soldier in the Roman army, and steal a toga without getting caught. If I do get caught, that's fine, all I have to do is fight 30,000 soldiers... win, change history, be hailed a **hero** and a leader, probably have a month named after me – TEDUARY or OCTEDBER – and then escape back to the present day... Easy.

Sorry, did I say easy? I meant really, *really*, REALLY <u>HARD</u>!

I had to think on my feet – which was a problem as I was sitting on my bum (with a spear pointing at my nose). I remembered reading somewhere that if you are in trouble, confusing the attacker will work.

Or, I might've just made that up...

Actually, thinking about it, I now seem to recall that if I was being attacked I should stand up, wave my arms around and make as much **noise** as possible.

Or that might only work when being attacked by bears... Yes, I'm sure it was something to do with bears. Or sharks, perhaps it was sharks?

Wait, wasn't I supposed to curl up in a ball?

No, I'm pretty sure that's only for lions...

Oh, why doesn't school ever teach the important, useful things, like what to do when being threatened by 30,000 Roman soldiers?

Oh, well, here goes nothing.

'Wait, wait,' I pleaded. 'I need to ask you one quick question.'

'A question? What question?' asked the angry soldier. He nodded to the other soldiers who moved their spears away from my nose.

'Do togas come in girl sizes? I think she's about a size 8 or 10? I'm not really sure and apparently it's rude to ask. Oh, and do they come in different colours?'

'What?' asked 30,000 soldiers. Being honest, only one of them said that, but I imagine 29,999 thought it.

'Girls wear tunics. Only Roman men wear togas. Now, guards, seize him!' The guards took a step forward, ready to grab me.

'Wait, wait, wait!' I pleaded, waving my arms around to slow them down. (They didn't immediately back off so I was right, that must've been bears.)

'You don't know where I can get one, do you?' I asked.

'What? A tunic? Rome, I presume.' The soldiers huddled together and whispered so I couldn't hear what they were saying. Eventually, they turned back AND I WAS GONE!

I'm kidding! I couldn't go back empty-handed, could I? No tunic meant no party. The things we do for *love*, eh?

'You are a very strange boy,' said the soldier. '*Very* strange indeed. When we have seized people in the past they have pleaded for us not to throw them in prison, kill them or turn them into slaves. As far as I or my men have known, no one has ever asked if we know where they can buy a toga.'

'Tunic,' I corrected.

'... or a tunic! I don't think you understand how much trouble you are in, young man. Being a Roman slave is a terrible, awful way to live. You will be nothing but the property of a rich Roman. You will have no rights and you will be forced to take on **back-breaking** work. You should be begging me to spare your life!'

'I know, I know and I *will* do the begging thing, I promise, but, before I do, can you just show me what a tunic looks like? Do you have one you could show me?'

'No!' boomed the soldier.

'Yes,' called one soldier from behind him.

'Really?' screamed the soldier.

'There's no need to scream,' I said.

'**SILENCE!** I'll scream if I want to scream!' screamed the soldier. He really liked screaming.

'Right, show the strange boy the tunic and then chain him up with the **slaves.** We will sell them to the highest bidder when we return to Rome,' he screamed even louder to the soldiers around him.

'You'll hurt your throat screaming like that,' I whispered.

'I'll hurt the end of your nose with

my **spear** if you don't shut up about my screaming. And then I'll chop off your arms and legs,' he whispered back.

'Fair enough,' I shrugged. 'You go ahead and scream all you like. I was just saying to your friend here how good you are at screaming. Probably the **best** screaming I've ever heard. In fact, if I'm being totally honest with you, I miss it when you *don't* scream,' I said, probably overdoing it a teeny, **tiny** bit.

The other soldier returned carrying the tunic. He held it out to me and I grabbed at it. He didn't let go.

I pulled a little.

He tugged it back.

I pulled.

He tugged.

He *really* didn't want to let go of it.

Neither did I.

'Oh, look over there. The BRITONS are coming!' I shouted as loud as I could.

All 30,000 men turned around. I grabbed the tunic, shut my eyes, held my breath, quickly raised my right arm and pumped it up and down really fast and repeated the word 'home' over and over again.

# CHAPTER 15

I slowly opened one eye and checked where I was. I breathed a sigh of relief when I recognised my surroundings. I'd done it. I was back in my bathroom. I had the tunic, I had my arms and legs still attached to my body and I had wet feet.

I made a promise to myself that I would never, ever rush back in time like that again. **TIME-TRAVELLING** needed careful planning to eliminate any kind of risk of personal injury, or who knows what might happen? In future, if *Chloe* wanted something then one way or another it would have to come from a shop, not from the past. Or, the next thing I'll know, she'll be demanding a pet dinosaur and I'd say, 'Of course, Chloe, I'll get you a pet dinosaur if you want a pet dinosaur. Here, I've got you a T-Rex. Do me a favour and point it at Sandy Bum, it looks hungry.'

The next morning, at school, I gave Chloe her tunic. She moaned a little that it wasn't a toga, and I told her that I'd travelled back over 2,000 years and had nearly been **enslaved** by the Roman army to get her that tunic and she should jolly well be grateful.

Actually, I didn't. I explained that girls wore tunics and that it was much more flattering and she'd look super cool in it.

That seemed to work. She was happy. I was happy. Everyone was happy.

Until that afternoon.

'Oh no!' cried Chloe. 'The party's been cancelled!'

I was not happy.

'Oh well, don't worry. Here,' she said, handing me the tunic. 'You can take it back to where you got it from if you want.'

'I don't think so,' I said, shaking my head.

'Why not? Didn't you keep the receipt?'

'No,' I said.

'Oh, where did you get it from?' she asked.

'ANCIENT ROME,' I laughed.

Chloe laughed too, clearly not believing me. 'Was it expensive?' she asked.

'It nearly cost me an arm and a leg,' I joked.

145

Chloe half-smiled. 'You really are *very* strange,' she said.

'So people keep telling me.'

'People? What people?' she asked.

'Romans mainly,' I replied. I walked off leaving her watching me and shaking her head in Confusion.

Well, that's it for now, but turn
the page for an exclusive
sneak preview of my next exciting
adventure!

First there's a bit to tell you
about what happens and then I'll let
you read the first chapter. FOR
FREE! The rest will be available
soon, but you'll have to buy that.
(How else am I going to afford to
buy Chloe chocolates and flowers?)

Enjoy!

# TED AND HIS TIME-TRAVELLING TOILET

## TUDOR TANGLE

When Ted finds out about the school prom he realises that for his one true love, Chloe Onions, to agree to go with him he has to impress her by learning to dance. So, he climbs into his toilet, flushes the chain and travels back to the 1500s where he meets keen dancer and chopping-people's-heads-off enthusiast, Henry VIII.

Can Ted convince the temperamental king to teach him to dance in time for the prom?

# CHAPTER 1

The class on stage had just finished their assembly telling the rest of the school how much they'd learned about butterflies (or, come to think of it, it might've been about Florence Nightingale or even about things you find in ponds – I wasn't really listening, and a quick glance around the hall showed me that neither was anyone else, including two teachers who had fallen asleep and were both **snoring** loudly). The class waited expectantly for a clap or at least some sort of acknowledgement, but the entire hall was silent, until one of the boys started picking his nose with great enthusiasm.

(When I say picking, he was digging like a pneumatic drill digs up a road.)

Giggling turned to laughter as he continued to dig further and further, deeper and deeper. I thought at one point, his finger was going to come wiggling out of his ear! Slowly but surely all the other students noticed and all the attention had turned from the other children on stage to the busy boy with a digit up his nostril. The giggling got louder and louder until eventually our head teacher Mr Munford stepped in.

'Well, what a fascinating assembly. We all enjoyed it and learned a lot about the pyramids of Egypt.'

Oh! It was about the pyramids of Egypt? I literally had no idea!

The head teacher continued, 'You've all worked very hard, and I think the whole school has learnted something new.'

'I didn't, but then I'm more... **picky**,' shouted Martin Harris, the school bully. **Everyone** laughed. Some because it was a funny thing to say given recent events, and some because they didn't want Martin to **PUNCH** them on the nose when he saw them next.

'Yes, thank you, Martin, you've earned yourself a **DETENTION** for shouting out!' snapped Mr Munford. Martin looked annoyed.

'Now, before you go back to class I have a couple of announcements to make. **Blah, blah, blah...**' He didn't actually say blah, blah, blah (although I wish he had – that would've been **brilliant!**). But, the things he said are not worth telling you (most of them were not worth telling me, and I go to that school!) But, then he surprised us all by finishing the assembly with a very interesting bit of information.

'... and that's why this year, for the first time in our school history, there will be a **prom.** There will be live music ...'

Everyone cheered.

'... there will be a photo booth ...'

Everyone cheered again.

'... and there will be excellent food provided by our school dinner ladies.' Everyone booed.

'That's enough. That's very **rude** of you all. Our dinner ladies work very hard to make sure you don't go hungry,' said Mr Munford.

'Well it looks like it hasn't worked for

him!' shouted Martin Harris, pointing to the nose-picking boy who was just removing his nose-picking finger from his mouth. **EWWWW!**

'Detention all this week, Martin!' **hollered** Mr Munford. 'Now all of you, go back to your classrooms quietly!'

We filed out of the hall making as much noise as we could. Because we are kids and it's what we do.

We all piled back into our classroom and waited for our teacher to follow. Someone called my name and I was just about to answer when...

HOLD IT! PAUSE THE STORY. NOBODY MOVE! EVERYONE STAY EXACTLY WHERE YOU ARE. BRACE YOURSELVES. SOMETHING INCREDIBLE IS ABOUT

TO HAPPEN!!!
READY?
OK, HERE IT IS...

**Chloe,** the best-looking girl in the school was walking towards me. Chloe and I had been getting on really well lately. I had to pause the story because, well if Chloe needs to speak to me then it's bound to be really important or maybe she just wants to hang out with me and chill out, you know? Hold on. Here she is now. Deep breath, here we go...

'Hey,' she says.
'Hey,' I replied.

... and she walked off.
Good, well that went well. Nice chat.

Friendly, upbeat. I admit it could've been a little more ... well, just a little more would've been better, but, you know ... I see it as a positive step in the right direction.

So, where was I before Chloe and I hung out?

(Who's laughing? Are you laughing? We spoke and for a few moments we hung out. So, technically I'm correct. WHO'S LAUGHING NOW, EH? Oh, it's still you.)

When you have finished laughing at me and are prepared to be *sensible* and accept that Chloe clearly likes me and that we are destined to be together, then you can come and join me at the beginning of the next chapter. Until then, you stay right here and think about your attitude.

# ABOUT THE AUTHOR

Steven Vinacour writes and directs TV shows and adverts and owns a content creation company, creating content for people who want content creating.

He likes skateboarding, dogs, magic, going to the gym, eating, and writing books about toilets (but not all at the same time).

He can't sing, plays football badly, his dancing abilities are questionable and he's not very good at being an adult.

Steven doesn't take life seriously enough and probably should know better.

# GET IN TOUCH!

Ted **loves** to hear from you. If there is something you really want to know, really, **really** want to ask or really, **really**, **really** want to tell him then send him an email, and as soon as he gets back from **TIME-TRAVELLING**, he'll reply.

**www.tedstoilet.co.uk**

Email: **tedstoilet@mail.com**

Or follow Steven Vinacour on Instagram where you'll find news, tour dates and silliness. **@stevenvinacourauthor**

Who knows? Maybe you'll see your message or question in a future story of

# READERS' THOUGHTS

"I loved the book. Ted is a very funny boy, and he has some very funny thoughts and says and does some very funny things, which made me laugh out loud so many times!" **Matthew**

Hi Matthew! Err.. when you say I'm a very 'funny' boy, you do mean I'm hilarious and witty, and not 'funny' as in strange and weird, don't you...? I hope so.

"I absolutely loved it. It was so so funny and I learned stuff too! I even wrote my own story about a time-travelling washing machine." **Amelie**

A time-travelling washing machine is a great idea. Travelling back in time and getting your clothes washed at the same time. What a brilliant idea, Amelie!

"I loved it when Ted stood up to a bully who made fun of him for wearing something he was proud to wear, just because it wasn't 'normal'!" **Kacey**

Thanks, Kacey. Who wants to be normal? Not me! My main mode of transport is a toilet and there's NOTHING normal about that!

"Ted's adventures are hilarious. The book has some fascinating facts, brilliant jokes and a bit of love. I loved it so much, I even memorised Ted's full name!!" **Joshua**

Hi Joshua, I must correct you on one thing. There isn't a 'bit' of love, there is a LOT of love. If Chloe reads this and sees there's only a 'bit' of love, she might lose interest in me and that would be a disaster! Glad you liked it (not as much as I like Chloe though).

# THANKS

Thanks to the team at Award Publications, especially Anna and Fiona, for loving and believing in Ted as much as I do. I can't thank them enough. Thanks to James Cottell too for the fab artwork.

A **BIG** thank you to my family, especially Jo, Chloe and Oliver for their continued love and support of my continual silliness.

(I was also going to thank my goldfish, Goldie, for always being happy, never arguing with me and always looking grateful when I feed him/her but I've just checked and he/she is floating upside down in the tank. The future is not looking good for Goldie. RIP, Goldie.)

And thanks to **you,** the reader, for choosing this book. If you've enjoyed it, then get in touch. I'd love to hear from you.